This book is for

_____ ,

who is just the cutest.

To sweet Emily Scanio—LHH

To my grandmas, Beba and Patti.
Thank you for encouraging me
to be an artist from that very first drawing
of a five-legged stick cat.—SH

Next to You

A Book of Adorableness

Lori Haskins Houran

pictures by
Sydney Hanson

Albert Whitman & Company
Chicago, Illinois

Next to you,
the softest puppy in the world
is only *kind of* cute.

Two kittens with a ball of yarn?

A line of fuzzy yellow ducklings?

A squirrel eating a doughnut
with his tiny hands?

Adorable, sure.
But next to you?
Meh. Just OK.

Take a baby chick.

Take a whole BASKET of baby chicks…

Add a piglet in a sweater,

a monkey sucking her thumb,

an elephant calf taking a bath,

a fawn trying to stand up for the first time,

a row of wee possums hanging upside down,

a yawning tiger cub,

and a bunny—the kind with
the little round fluffy tail.

Pretty irresistible, right?
But next to you...
Whatever.

Lambs. Pandas.
Koalas. Penguins.

Cute, cute, cute,

and cute.

Until you came along.
Now?
Sorta so-so.

A newborn giraffe—
Oh, wait. Hang on.
I didn't realize newborn giraffes were
SO. UNBELIEVABLY. SWEET.

I mean, have you *seen* one?
Awwww.

They might be…
it's possible that they're—
No! NO WAY!
They are NOT as adorable as you.
Not NEARLY.

Next to you,
even a baby *seal*
doesn't stand a chance.
And you know what?

I'm happy to be...
next to you.

Library of Congress Cataloging-in-Publication
data is on file with the publisher.

Text copyright © 2016 by Lori Haskins Houran
Pictures copyright © 2016 by Albert Whitman & Company
Pictures by Sydney Hanson
Published in 2016 by Albert Whitman & Company
ISBN 978-0-8075-5600-9

Printed in China
10 9 8 7 6 5 4 3 2 1 HH 24 23 22 21 20 19 18 17 16 15

Design by Jordan Kost

For more information about Albert Whitman & Company,
visit our web site at www.albertwhitman.com.